Nutik & Amaroq

JEAN CRAIGHEAD GEORGE

Play Ball

ILLUSTRATED BY **TED RAND**

HARPERCOLLINS*PUBLISHERS*

Library of Congress Cataloging-in-Publication Data George, Jean Craighead, date Nutik & Amaroq play ball / Jean Craighead George ; illustrated by Ted Rand. p. cm. Summary: While searching for a missing football, a young Eskimo boy and his wolf pup friend nearly get lost on the tundra. ISBN 0-06-028166-9. – ISBN 0-06-028167-7 (lib. bdg.) 1. Eskimos–Juvenile fiction. [1. Eskimos–Fiction. 2. Wolves–Fiction. 3. Arctic regions–Fiction.] I. Title. II. Rand, Ted, ill. III. Nutik and Amaroq play ball.
PZ7.G2933Nu 2001 99-10505 [E]–dc21 CIP AC Typography by Matt Adamec 1 2 3 4 5 6 7 8 9 10 ❖ First Edition

To Sam
–J.C.G.

To Robert Gleason,
a friend who knows the Arctic
–T.R.

Amaroq was a lively little Eskimo boy who had a beautiful wolf pup named Nutik. Amaroq was named for a great wolf leader. Nutik was the great leader's grandpup. He and the boy were like brothers.

It was the time of day the two played football.

But today they couldn't play.

Their football was gone.

It had disappeared after the Kuklook boys, the pranksters of Kangit village, had dropped by for a visit.

"What shall we do?" asked Amaroq.

Nutik picked up a boot and brought it to Amaroq.

"You want to go outside?"

Nutik wagged his tail to say "Yes" in wolf talk.

Amaroq put on his mud boots and lightweight parka.

They stepped into the puddle-glorious world of the summer Arctic, where the sun shines all day and all night.

"Do you want to splash in the mucky pools?" Amaroq asked. Nutik did not wag his tail.

Nutik ran to the edge of the Avalik River, which ran by their house.

"You want to fish?"

Nutik did not wag his tail.

He trotted to the sealskin boat.

"You want to go whaling?" the boy asked.

Nutik lifted his tail, but he did not wag it.

Nutik sniffed in all directions. His nose quivered in excitement.

Gulls soared overhead, and snowbirds sang like piccolos.

Nutik bounced up on his back feet and dashed to the schoolhouse.

"I know what you want to do," Amaroq said when he got there. "You want to go to school."

Nutik's tail still did not wag.

"Well, what do you want to do?" Amaroq asked.

Nutik whimpered to say "Come with me." They ran to the airplane hangar. Amaroq's father, Kapugen, kept his plane there.

"You want to fly?" the boy asked, and chuckled.

Nutik held his fluffy full tail very still. He did not want to fly. He ran to the fish-drying racks. He sniffed here and there, then set out across the vast, treeless tundra.

"Ee-lie," said Amaroq. "You want to take a walk. Let's go."

They walked and walked.

The day was warm for the Arctic, and clear.

The grasses whistled, and the frozen earth tinkled as it thawed.

Nutik sniffed the air and trotted east.

Then he sniffed the air and trotted south.

They walked through moss and inch-high yellow flowers.

They strode up and down winter's frost heaves.

Finally Amaroq stopped and looked around.

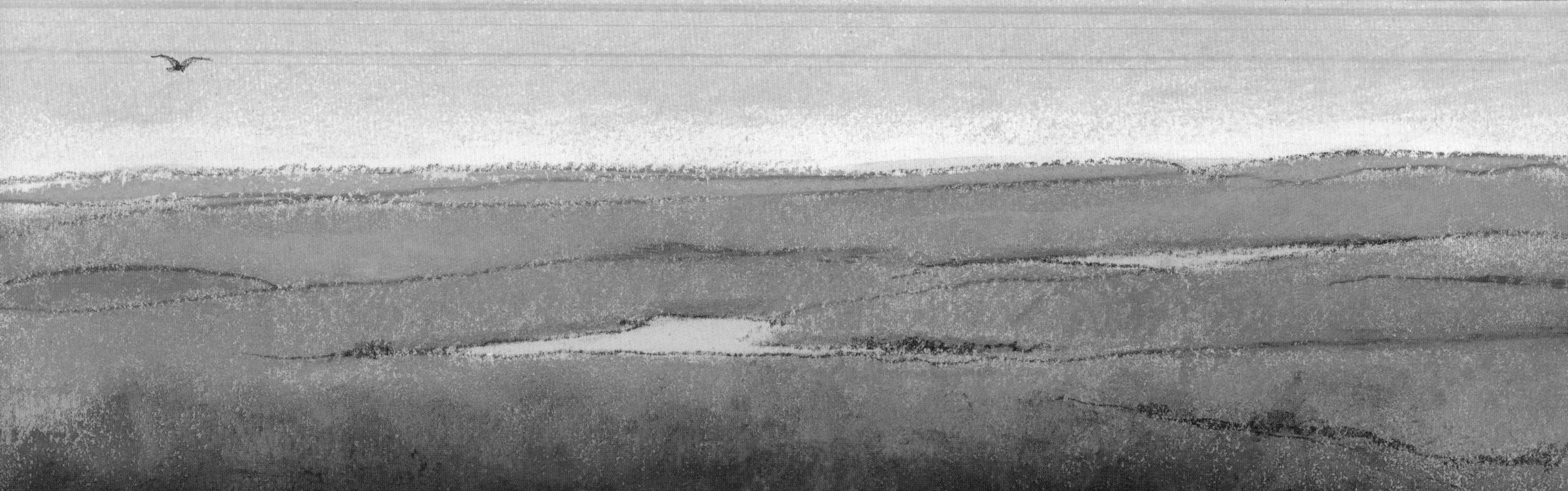

He could not see his village.

He could not see the fish-drying racks.

He could not see his father's airplane hangar.

He could not see the school.

"We are lost," he said, and his voice trembled. He was very frightened. He could see no landmarks, no pathways. He shut his eyes tightly and wondered what the wolf Amaroq would do.

The great wolf leader, he remembered, would have observed nature and followed what it said.

Amaroq, too, would observe nature. He, too, would follow what it said.

Amaroq observed the gulls flying through the morning light. They were going to the fish-drying racks to eat discarded bits of fish. He would follow them and be home. He felt fine again.

He ran after Nutik. The wolf pup came to a halt at a den.

"Ee-lie," Amaroq said. "Is that what you want to do? Play with tough little wolverine pups?"

But Nutik did not wag his tail. He trotted on.

Now it was noon. Amaroq was hungry.

His father, Kapugen, had taught him to keep a fish line in his pocket. If he got hungry, he could always catch a fish. He stopped at a lake to catch their lunch.

But Nutik ran on. He didn't want lunch.

Amaroq wound in his line and ran after him.

They came to an empty oil barrel. A fox ran out from behind it.

"A fox," said Amaroq. "Is that what you want to do–chase a fox?"

Nutik did not wag his tail.

He sniffed into a big hole in the barrel. He nudged Amaroq's hand with his cool, moist nose.

"I know what you want," said Amaroq. "There's something in that barrel. You want me to stick my hand in and get it."

At last Nutik wagged his tail.

"Suppose there is a weasel in there. He'll bite me," said Amaroq.

Nutik wagged his tail harder.

"Suppose there is a grizzly cub in there. He'll claw me."

Nutik opened his mouth and pulled back his lips in a wolf smile.

"Is something good inside?"

Nutik wagged his tail.

"All right," said Amaroq. "I'll do it. Then we can go home."

Amaroq held his breath. He thought of Amaroq, the brave wolf. Closing his eyes, he reached into the barrel. It was cold inside. Nothing stirred.

Nothing bit. Nothing clawed.

His hand touched a smooth object. He pulled it out.

"Our football!" he cried. "Those Kuklook boys hid it way out here. No wonder I couldn't find it. But you did, Nutik. Ee-lie, what a good nose you have."

Amaroq threw his arms around the furry neck. "Now we can go home and play football."

But Nutik slapped the ground with his front paws to say "Let's play now."

"I can't play now," Amaroq said. "I have to observe the gulls and find our way home."

Nutik pranced and danced so joyfully, Amaroq couldn't resist. He would play now and observe later.

With a big smile he kicked the ball to Nutik.

The wolf pup pounced on the ball. He took it in his teeth and ran. Amaroq tackled him, got the ball, and ran. Nutik chased him.

Amaroq and Nutik rolled and tackled, chased and kicked. Nutik growled his friendship growl. Amaroq shouted in joy. He completely forgot how hungry he was. The boy and the wolf pup played for a long, long time.

Finally Amaroq tucked the ball under his arm and stood up. He observed the sky. The gulls were flying overhead. He led off in the direction they were going.

Nutik did not follow him. He woofed and trotted in the opposite direction.

"No," Amaroq called. "We have to go home now. Follow me."

Amaroq walked a few steps and stopped. If Nutik's wonderful nose could find the football that was so far away, Nutik could smell the way home. Amaroq turned and followed Nutik, and soon they were home.

At the fish rack Amaroq saw why he had been wrong. The morning had turned to afternoon. In the mornings gulls fly away from their roosts to eat. In the afternoons they fly back. The gulls Amaroq was following were going home to roost—away from the fish racks at Kangit village. If he had gone with them, he would surely have been lost on the tundra. Amaroq gave Nutik a grateful pat on his soft, fuzzy head.

Near the schoolhouse Amaroq smelled his mother's cooking.

"Do you want to eat, Nutik?"

Nutik wagged his tail twice. They ran side by side, woofing and laughing.

Inside the house they sat down to a very late dinner, although the sun was shining brightly in the sky. It shone down on the oil barrel. It shone down on the fish racks. It shone down on the airplane hangar and schoolhouse. And it shone down on all the intelligent living things at the top of the world.